matriarchs

a little book of heresies

Published November 2016

malkapoet.blogspot.com
malkapoet@gmail.com

Book and cover design by Aline Talatinian
Cover photograph iStockphoto/Ridofranz

ISBN 978-87-994475-6-5

matriarchs

a little book of heresies

Marlene R. Edelstein

Contents

Foreword

The Matriarchs and Patriarchs of the Bible who are celebrated as exemplary characters especially favoured by the Almighty are conventionally Sarah and Abraham, their son Isaac and his wife Rebecca, and their son Jacob with his wives Rachel and Leah. Reading the text of the Bible, however, leaves one with the impression that biblical characters are all too human, and their humanity is one of the things I want to stress in these stories.

But I have further aims than simply to compose realistic narratives. I have attempted to create a number of different female voices in order to bring out meanings which are only latent in the familiar biblical narratives. Furthermore, I have expanded the term 'matriarch' to include other female characters: Bilhah and Zilpah, the concubines who gave birth to four of Jacob's son's, Deborah who is called "a mother in Israel", Ruth who is the foremother of King David, and the Virgin Mary. The last story, 'Martha's Tale', expands on the episode in Luke 10 which contrasts the characters of Mary and Martha, the sisters of Lazarus; although Martha, unlike the protagonists of the previous stories, is not important as a mother, I use her as the exemplar of a new kind of female life and devotion.

My female characters are presented as trapped in the exigencies of a patriarchal culture which in general they are unable to analyse, let alone resist, though some of my matriarchs occasionally have rebellious or visionary insights despite their unquestioning acceptance of the cultural norms. I have also used midrashic sources to expose the obstinately androcentric nature of the tradition which brings these female characters to us.

My matriarchs are trapped not only in the assumptions of their own culture but in the finality of familiar tales, so in some instances dramatic irony operates: the reader has knowledge of future outcomes which is unavailable to the characters. If we accept that the Bible is the word of God we may discern in it the working-out of an inscrutable plan which transcends the fate of individual lives; if we regard it as a volume put together by human redactors another kind of determinism applies to its characters. The stories centred on Deborah and Ruth explore this dimension of the Bible as a text, whether of divine or human authorship.

These stories are essentially works of fiction based on the biblical text, which they present from new angles, with changes of emphasis and occasional elision or rearrangement of details. Though they are imbued with a controlling underlying concept, they do not make up one consistent narrative: reality is multifaceted and truth is a slippery concept. A three-year debate in Talmudic times on the conflicting views on Jewish law of the two major schools of Hillel and Shammai was settled by this verdict from Heaven: both are the word of the living God. The Talmud is an endless process of interpretation and discovery; so, I modestly suggest, is the creative imagination as it expands in line with the evolution of experience.

My deepest gratitude to Aline Talatanian for her great technical expertise in designing this book, and for her patience with my many changes of mind, and to Hannah Bubandt for proof reading the text so scrupulously and efficiently

Marlene R. Edelstein, Copenhagen, January 2014

A Note on Names

In general I use the familiar English versions of biblical names, with, however, these exceptions. Rebecca is referred to throughout by her Hebrew name Rivka, except once by herself, at the start of her story. She regards the name Rebecca as signifying a modern, liberated mode of being which she longs to attain but never can: she is doomed to remain Rivka. In the first story Isaac is called by his Hebrew name Yitzchak, cognate with the word meaning 'to laugh', though in all subsequent mentions he is called Isaac. Though it may seem confusing at first reading, I have opted for this to indicate a rupture between the happy laughing little boy Yitzchak romping around the women's tents and the adult patriarch Isaac, broken in body and spirit after the trauma of the sacrifice in Moriah.

Please note: for traditional reasons the name Deborah is used not only for the great warlike Judge but also for two nurses, subsidiary characters who are only mentioned. And naturally, Mary the sister of Martha is not identical with Mary the Mother of Jesus, who is himself referred to as Josh, the shortened version of his Hebrew name Joshuah .

Part One

In the Beginning

Nameless

C hildren are naturally women's business. We birth them, suckle them, do our best to keep them from harm, soothe them when they fall and put up with their screaming. We comfort each other when our infants die. Men have more important matters to think about, so we're reluctant to disturb them with chatter about pregnancy and its terrors. If we miscarry, or the baby is born dead, or a girl, we talk about it among ourselves and console each other, but our husbands needn't know of it. It's only necessary to present them with healthy, thriving sons.

Abraham's daughters romped around the tents, indistinguishable to him from the daughters of his servants and herdsmen. Every now and again he needed a girl for a bride as part of a trade deal, purchasing favour as well as merchandise from surrounding tribal lords: as itinerant foreigners our situation was precarious. Then he would march over to the women's tents and inspect the blooming maidens, demanding "Which of these are mine?". Not that it made any difference – he was only vaguely aware of his female offspring, and we could have pushed forward any of the girls. Once, indeed, when Sarah was reluctant to part so soon with Abigail, her witty favourite, we substituted a girl of

6

lower birth, and as there was no call for her to speak nobody suspected. She was happy enough to be decked out in jewels and fine linen. We loaded her onto the camel with the other gifts and that was the last we saw of her. It was always the same: our daughters shared our work and our festivals, they learnt our mysteries, but to the men they were merely tokens of exchange. Such is the way of the world. For this reason we also longed for sons, who would be kept in the family; even after they were full grown we could watch their progress and celebrate their achievements, if from a distance.

It was vital for Abraham to have sons. Only a son could receive the blessing, only a son could transmit the Covenant to future generations. There were solemn ceremonies for the birth of a son, welcoming him into the family, into the tribe and into the human race. He would be given a name to make him an individual, a name which would be remembered, recorded and referred to for eternity. So Sarah's inability to produce a living son was a blemish, a failing. Despite her numerous pregnancies, miscarriages, stillbirths and four fine daughters who at the time this incident took place were grown women, married, and for all we knew mothers themselves, she was castigated as barren. That shameful episode of Hagar and the son who was meant to make up for Sarah's failure only made things worse for her.

We were a self-contained little community, keeping to ourselves and rarely receiving visitors. The arrival of strangers was felt to be rather ominous. At best it called for complicated rituals of hospitality, and there was the perpetual risk that seemingly innocuous travellers were spies, the advance guard of a marauding nation. And there was something uncanny about these strangers who materialised without warning out of the heat haze.

It's a moot point whether they were real living men, spiritual entities or figments of Abraham's imagination. They certainly came at an inconvenient moment. Following a séance with his God in which he was once again promised a multitude of descendants, Abraham had very recently circumcised himself and the other males of our settlement, apparently in acknowledgement of this covenant, and it was taking him some time to get over the operation; after all, he was nearly a hundred years old. He was sitting in the shade at the entrance to his tent at the hottest time of the day, probably dozing as elderly people do on sultry afternoons, when he saw, at a short distance from himself, what looked like three men, though their number isn't certain: sometimes the story is told as if there was only one of them, sometimes with three fluctuating into one. We all know the tricks your eyes can play on you if it's very hot and dry and you're in pain.

We only have Sarah's account to go by, and she had to rely on what Abraham told her, because she couldn't really see what was going on as she was listening from behind the flap at the entrance to the tent. She heard mysterious mumblings, but couldn't swear to how many voices there were. Maybe her husband was simply muttering to himself? But no, there seemed to be a strange voice saying that she, Sarah, would soon be a mother! Try as she might, she couldn't keep herself from bitter laughter, but when Abraham pushed her outside, demanding to know what she found so amusing and telling her angrily that God had assured him that she'd bear a son in the following year, she was torn between ridicule and terror. She was then 90 and long past childbearing. "I didn't laugh", she quavered, but it was futile. Abraham had heard her, and so had whoever might have been with him in the tent.

Sore and weary though he was, Abraham insisted on spending the night in her tent doing the Lord's work, and sure enough, improbable though it sounds, a few weeks later Sarah suspected and feared that she had indeed conceived. We were all aghast. Naturally her menstruation had ceased decades before, so the signs of pregnancy were unclear until the baby quickened within her shrivelled body. We were sitting among the tents grinding beans for the pot when she suddenly jerked and flinched, then laughed bitterly. "Now that I'm worn out", she exclaimed, "shall I have my heart's desire?"

Through the remaining months we took care of her, sharing her tasks among us so as not to add to the unnatural burden she was carrying. We also shared her unspoken dread of the looming birth.

I hope never to experience a confinement like that one again. I was one of the few old enough to have ministered to Sarah at the birth of her daughters and at her failed pregnancies, and my heart was wrenched as that old woman, the lady of our settlement, our princess, for hours on end exerted superhuman strength to bring her son into the world. When it was all over she sank into exhausted slumber and we took up the undersized, feebly mewling little boy to wash and swaddle him before presenting him triumphantly to his overjoyed father.

For Abraham, though, the time for rejoicing came eight days later when he solemnly circumcised the boy. Miraculously, Sarah's milk had arrived on cue and the child had thrived. In her relief at having been spared to attain the highest purpose of her existence Sarah again laughed and said, "God has given me laughter. All who hear about it will laugh for me. Who would have even suggested to Abraham that Sarah would be nursing children? But here I have given birth to a son in his old age"[1]. For once Abraham listened to her and named the boy Yitzchak, laughter, at his circumcision.

When Yitzchak was weaned Abraham gave a great feast for the men, to mark the day on which his son left the women's world behind. But of course the boy still spent a lot of his time among the women's tents running around with the children of the slaves, his half-sisters and cousins, and the others whose names will not be recorded. He was a happy, laughing boy, everyone's darling, and especially petted and indulged because he was often somewhat sickly: we almost lost him a couple of times.

But these days he's more and more with Abraham, learning to be a man, and now we rarely see him among us. Poor boy – he respects his father, of course, as is only right, but he's truly attached to his mother and to all us older aunties, as he calls us. What kind of a man will he make? He's almost grown now, and soon his father will be looking out for a wife for him, a political alliance no doubt. Well, whatever girl he brings us from her home and her friends, the boy has a loving heart, and we'll welcome her and teach her to become one of us.

Sarah's sitting outside her tent waiting, as women often do. She's growing increasingly uneasy. A couple of days ago, without any warning, Abraham took Yitzchak into the mountains with him to make sacrifice to his inscrutable deity. Sarah grew pale with terror; and we remembered her reputation as a prophetess. They ought to be back any time now. We're doing our best to laugh her out of her apprehensions, but her anxiety is starting to infect us too.

---

1 *Genesis 21:6-7*

Her Egyptian Maidservant

It seemed like a good idea at the time, though in fact I had niggling doubts which I did my best to hide from myself. Sometimes I was tangled up in emotions like those I had known in my youth when the seers chanted tales of the gods and our ancestors, or when the women whispered news of marriage and childbearing.

Naturally I kept these vague fears to myself. It was such a relief that he was no longer glooming about the fields and tents, shooting accusatory glances at me whenever our paths crossed. As if it was my fault. I had done everything a wife could or should – lain naked in the glow of the full moon, swallowed disgusting potions brewed before dayrise by the medicine woman, hid mandrakes in my bed on the nights he visited me. I implored teeming mothers to touch and bless me. Sometimes it seemed as if my prayers were answered. I'd go about my usual business gingerly, hopefully – and suddenly my womb would open to eject what was never meant to be.

As years passed my heart grew crabbed with bitterness and disappointment. Proudly I showed nothing of this, holding myself stiffly erect as befits my status in the community. Not so Abram; he muttered imprecations. A few times he came to my tent and coupled with me violently, so that I could feel his hatred, wrenching my arms and face, shaming me with unnatural, forbidden acts, bruising my body's soft secrets. In the morning I was sore and almost lame, but I kept silent. After all, we were both suffering.

The time came when there was nothing more to hope for. I would never give Abram the live progeny he yearned for so desperately and hoped for so irrationally. Was his God laughing up his sleeve, imposing this misery on us after having promised my husband that he would derive a great nation from us? We were in deadlock, the burden of my barrenness crushing our life-force.

But one day the gloom began to disperse. My maidservant was oiling and braiding my hair, and the gentle fluttering of her fingers on my scalp and my neck suddenly teased out the idea. The promise had been given to Abram, not to me. I need not be the woman who bore his children. The solution was right there.

Hagar was a princess in her own right, the daughter of the Pharaoh with whom Abram was involved in a web of misunderstandings when we were in Egypt. When she had seen the might of Abram's God she chose to return for us. "I'd rather be a slave in Sarai's house than a princess in my father's", she had said, or something along those lines. So my slave was what she was, my property, and as is the case with slaves any children she bore would be my property too, my children in fact, if I chose. Furthermore, I had heard tell of a ritual which cemented the transfer of motherhood, though I'd never known it to be practised before. This is what we could do: she would position herself between my open thighs, my knees supporting the back of hers, and so Abram would impregnate her. It was as if he was coupling with me, with her as proxy.

As soon as the opportunity arouse I broached the matter with my husband. His eyes lit up. Not only, I suspect, from the renewed hope of offspring, but in anticipation of intimate knowledge of the beautiful Egyptian. Abram was basically a good man. He could have lain with her at any time, but he had always remained faithful to me, even renouncing the privilege of lying with the slave-girls. But this was another matter. It was my suggestion, and a custom hallowed by ancient practice.

So, in the semi-darkness of the nuptial tent, I lounged on rich woven blankets, my back supported by many royal cushions, my legs sprawled open to accommodate Hagar's warm weight as Abram thrust into her. It wasn't the most comfortable of positions, in more than one respect. To steady us, I clasped my arms around her body, cupping her breasts as firmly as I could, my fingers aware of their softness beneath the fine linen of her tunic. In a way, we were alone there, we two women, with Abram merely an external force welding us together. A thought swam across my mind – *why should men have all this pleasure?* And I was assaulted by an army of emotions – jealousy, envy, desire, terror.

. . . .

They didn't ask my permission. I didn't protest, but I was still outraged, humiliated. They had never given me a husband. No brisk and beautiful young man had ever pleasured me in the secrecy of my tent. Instead, my body was penetrated by my old mistress's old husband. I was used for breeding, like a ewe or a heifer. But the child would be mine, despite their mumbo-jumbo.

Because there would be a child. Abram wasn't infertile, she was the defective one. As my belly swelled I refused to do heavy work because of my condition, and she eyed me with hatred. She turned against that malleable husband of hers, saying I was insubordinate and scornful, and it was all his doing. Surreptitiously she'd slap me, try to trip me up, set me impossible tasks, and when I merely turned away from her in disdain she hurled curses at me.

The day came when I could stand it no longer. I left the encampment and went out into the desert until I found a spring, where I sat down to weep and think. What I intended to do I cannot say. I knew I must either return or perish, but for the moment I needed to be quiet and alone. Gradually I became aware of a presence, like a rippling in the moment of being. I looked up timidly and saw, or rather sensed, a radiance, and words pierced my ears. "Hagar, slave of Sarai, where have you come from, and where are you going?"

I answered, "I'm running away from my mistress Sarai," though I knew there was no need, convinced as I was that this could only be an angel of the Lord.

Then the angel told me to return to my mistress and submit to her, and when he added, "I will increase your descendants so much that they will be too numerous to count" I knew that the promise Abram had been given depended on me. What the angel said next was hard to comprehend, as prophesies tend to be:

"You are now pregnant, and you will give birth to a son. You shall name him Ishmael, for the LORD HAS HEARD OF YOUR MISERY. He will be a wild donkey of a man; his hand will be against everyone and everyone's hand against him, and he will live in hostility toward all his brothers."

I went back – what else was there for me to do? My absence had scared Sarai, so from then on then on she behaved towards me decently, and I comported myself meekly. I never told her about my experience in the desert.

......

It didn't turn out in the way I'd imagined. Now she had a son, and I didn't. She suckled the child and he was still part of her. Whenever I saw them together I was mad with irritation. It was no help that Abram was besotted by the child, "Ishmael, Ishmael", he'd croon, "my boy, my son, my nation". For years I no longer had a role in his scheme of things.

All this changed with the three eerie visitors with their incredible prediction that I, 90-year-old Sarah (since, for some unfathomable reason they'd changed our names) would at last become a mother, and that it was from my son that Abraham, as I now had to call him, would become the father of multitudes. The situation was totally different, and once my Isaac was born my mind was made up. Why should I suffer the insolence of that hussy and the constant screaming and defiance of her brat any longer? He was almost fully grown and completely unmanageable. Soon they'd be looking for a wife for him and Abraham would be drooling over his grandchildren. I confronted my husband and insisted that they should be thrown out.

Of course he resisted, he demurred. How could I even consider treating my own family so cruelly, so heartlessly? He wept, a ridiculous old man with tears trickling down his wrinkled cheeks. Hagar wept, prostrating herself before me, kissing my feet. But despite the wound it inflicted on my heart, I was unrelenting. And for once Abraham's God was on my side.

I kept out of the way when they left. I prepared food for them myself, and skins of water, and I suspect that Abraham gave her plenty of money. But what good would money be to them in the desert?

......

I will never forget that God spoke to me twice. He came to me again as I wept in the desert, convinced that my son was dying and that I would follow him soon. "Come, lift up the boy and hold him by the hand", he urged me, "for I will make a great nation of him". When I opened my eyes I perceived a well of water which surely had not been there before. God has shown me by his mercies and his graciousness that Ishmael is his chosen one.

In his heart Abraham thought so too. When the angels came with the news that ancient Sarah would bear him a son his first incredulous reaction was to implore that Ishmael might live in the presence of God. And after we were resettled in the wilderness of Paran, making a bleak living by gathering dates and olives and herding camels, Abraham would visit us as often as his business and advanced age would permit him to do so. Sarah couldn't prevent him from seeing his son, though he had to be diplomatic about it to maintain peace in the home. "I won't even get off my camel", he would promise her, "just see him and speak a few words".

I know these things because after Sarah died I became Abraham's second wife, the woman he could share his innermost thoughts with. There's one secret I'm sure he never confided to anyone else, and certainly not to Sarah: when God demanded his beloved son as a sacrifice he was bewildered by uncertainty, unable to protest and negotiate. Which of his sons was meant? He would have been less able to give up Ishmael than that feeble child of an aged jealous mother.

Abraham is gone now, carrying his guilt and horror to the grave. When his servant brought us the news of his death Ishmael went straight to Isaac and together they buried their father. For one part of the prophesy hasn't come true: the two brothers are not enemies, Ishmael still associates Isaac with that sweet baby he used to cuddle and sing to. And I'm a matriarch, as Sarah never was – so let them be friends.

Rivka

My name's Rivka, but you can call me Rebecca. It sounds more modern, more the kind of woman I'd like to be, if only I'd had the chance. I've always been restless, as if I really belonged in some other place and time, and if I just tried hard, used my brain a little more intensely, I'd be able to get there. Some crazy people believe that your soul wanders from one life to another; well, I was desperate to escape from this life and was always on the lookout for an escape route, a crack in the world which I could slip through into freedom and fulfilment.

You can't imagine the tedium of my early youth in Aram. I felt I was destined for fame, but hanging around at home, never going anywhere but to the well to fetch water, wouldn't help me achieve it. It was alright for my twin brother Laban. He'd be in charge of the property and the family business eventually, so it wasn't long before he was learning the tricks of the trade and being included as a grown man at all the dinners and discussions. I knew I was at least as clever as him, and nothing like as lazy, but I was expected to be meek and dutiful, with nothing to look forward to but a marriage of alliance to some patriarchal half-wit and no say in the deal. So as I went about meekly doing what was expected of me, my mind was turning over schemes to get as much control of my life as was feasible. But women have to be realistic. They may nurture a visionary project, just as men do, but few have the courage and intelligence to get themselves even halfway to their goal. I would have to marry, no avoiding that, but I prayed for a husband I could manage and influence.

So there I was again, at the eternal schlepp to the well for water, the big jar balanced on my hypocritical head. I slipped it down beside the well and was just lifting it up to be filled when I caught sight of something that made my heart jump – a caravan of ten camels led by a venerable-looking foreigner! Something was happening at last. Maybe my wishes were starting to come true; but I'd have to play my cards right.

In fact everything followed as if predestined. The foreigner came over to me and said, "Please, let me sip a little water from your jar". "Drink, my lord", I replied, and he took much more than just a sip. He must have been on the road a long time and exhausted his water supply. The thought slipped into my head to offer to draw water for his camels too, and not waiting for an answer I emptied the jar into the drinking trough and ran back to the well to get more. It's a good thing I was young and fit: there were ten camels, all with hollow sides, so I had to fill that trough over and over again.

It paid off, though. When the camels had at last drunk their fill the man reached into one of the saddle-bags and presented me with a gold nose-ring weighing at least a half-shekel and two hefty gold arm-bands. My true worth was being acknowledged! He asked me then about my family, and if there was room in our house for him to spend the night there. He enquired whose daughter I was. I was a little annoyed that he didn't start by asking me my name, but I thought it best to tread carefully. I gave him the information he wanted, making sure though that I slipped in the name of my grandmother Milcah, and assured him that we had plenty of provision for himself and the camels. When the man bowed down in homage to his God I really pricked up my ears: "Blessed be the Lord, the God of my master Abraham, who has not withheld His steadfast faithfulness from my master. For I have been guided on my errand by the Lord, to the house of my master's kinsmen".

I was stunned. I knew that we had kinsfolk who had left this country long ago; I'd heard tell of a kind of great-uncle of mine called Abram – could this Abraham be a relative of his? Whoever he was, he was clearly extremely wealthy. As I found out later, Abram and Abraham were one and the same person, so we were indeed family.

I ran to my mother's house to announce the great news, and everyone started getting busy, as I knew they would. Ceremonial speeches of welcome, bathing of feet, feeding of camels, and of course food and drink – they were all rolled out over the course of the next few hours. If the stranger had been desperately hungry, he would have starved to death before the meal appeared, but when it did he insisted on telling his tale before touching the food.

As I listened, I was thankful that our customs dictated that my eyes should be modestly lowered, as surely they were sparkling with glee. In his sing-song formal way he first detailed the riches which Abraham had acquired – through the favour of his God, naturally – and how his wife had only borne one son, and that when they were both old. Now he was looking for a wife for the boy, but had taken the fancy to find one among the kinsfolk he had abandoned years and years before rather than marry into a local family. So Eliezer, Abraham's servant – which is what the stranger was, though to me he looked like a magnifico – was on a mission to find a suitable bride for his master's son. And my conduct, and of course my beauty, together with some occult signs, had convinced him that I was the girl!

My father and brother concurred that this matter was decreed, so there was nothing to discuss. Take her and go! At that, the stranger brought out rich garments and all kinds of objects made of gold and silver and presented them to me, with a deep bow, and then gave gifts to my brother and my mother. It was like a dream. Things were happening with a kind of inevitability, as if I had an important role to play, as I'd always suspected. When I'd got up that morning I had no idea that this would be anything but an ordinary uneventful day, like all the others I'd had to drag myself through, but at last my real life was starting.

The next day my stomach was turning over with nervousness. I couldn't eat, but my resolution was still firm. The man wanted us to leave immediately, despite my mother's protests that I should be allowed to stay with the family for ten more days. She must have known she'd never see me again. However, when they called for me and asked, "Will you go with this man?" I looked her straight in the eye and said "I will". I could see the distress in her face. She insisted though that my old nurse Deborah should accompany me, saying, "Soon, please God, when you become a mother yourself, you'll be grateful to have a woman you know with you", and added, "You'll also be glad not to be alone with those rough camel drivers", and of course she was right. My defiance was already crumbling, but I refused to show how shaky I felt.

The journey was hot and scary. Getting away from home didn't bring the sense of release that I'd imagined. The camel-drivers were wild men, and I flinched each time one of them leered at me. Luckily they were in awe of Eliezer, and Deborah seemed quite equal to their coarse banter. I'd never been up on a camel before, and the tossing and rocking, the terror of slipping off, kept me feeling sick most of the time. I was also wondering what I had let myself in for. What kind of a husband was I taking on? That window of opportunity I'd longed for now gaped vertiginously. During a merciful pause in our journey I timidly tried to find out a little about my prospective bridegroom. I learnt that he was called Isaac. He was an only child, and his mother had died recently. I already knew that his father had taken charge of his marriage. I began to cheer up and feel that my situation might be rather advantageous. I would be the principal woman in the family, and my husband was used to being managed.

That night, though, I was visited by a terrifying vision. I saw a bleak terrain beneath a fierce sky, solid with lowering reddish light. In this ghastly glow an old man held a long-bladed knife over a young lad lashed to a spar of rock and then plunged it down and in repeatedly with savage determination. I could hear no sound from them, neither speech nor screams, but from the sky came an inhuman rumbling noise: Anochi! Anochi![2] The desert night was cold, but I awoke sticky with terror.

Evening was coming on when we arrived at the region of the Negev which was our destination, and through the failing light I discerned an eerie apparition lolloping alone in the field. Was he one of the walking dead from stories which scare children? "That's my master's son", said Eliezer, in answer to my enquiring glance, and my nausea intensified to blinding giddiness. To keep myself from falling off the camel I descended from it gingerly and covered myself with my veil, ostensibly in modesty but in truth in a feeble attempt to protect myself from my fate.

---

2 *Hebrew for "I! I!": Anochi is the intensive form of the first-person singular pronoun,* ani.

Love Story

Wwhat do I remember? Days melt dreamily into each other for women who have only known one home, and it's only since we left that I've tried to recapture those youthful days. Well, I remember going out to the pasture to watch the sheep, and then herding them to the well so that they could drink after the parching day. That was always my job, whilst Leah brought in vegetables and herbs for the cooking pot. I remember too my father bewailing his hard lot of having only daughters. Once when travellers stopped at our encampment for food and rest they brought news of my aunt Rivka, who had left long before I was born to marry a rich cousin she'd never seen. She had twin sons, the travellers said, and after that my father was sure that we two girls were destined to marry them. He would have to make do with his sister's sons, if that's all the gods would grant him. So this is what I remember, the awareness that I was waiting for the winds of destiny to waft my fated husband to me. Whenever two strangers appeared travelling together we couldn't help wondering if they were Rivka's twins, come to claim their brides. We giggled about that, me and Leah, in the happy ignorance of maidenhood.

Jacob arrived by himself, though. I was taking the sheep down to the well and there he stood, conversing with the shepherds of three other flocks which were waiting to be watered. I took no heed of him, as he was alone and I was on the look-out for two men, but when he glanced at me joy and amazement lit up his face. His whole body quivered and seemed to glow with spiritual radiance. In one violent impulse he rolled the stone from the mouth of the well singlehandedly, a feat which normally required three or four men heaving together. He was a hero, and I had seen him before Leah did. As my sheep wobbled over to the well to drink he turned to me and kissed me, his cheeks wet with tears. "I'm Jacob, Rivka's son", he whispered bashfully. Where's your brother? I wondered, but didn't inquire – it's best for young girls not to ask questions or make demands. Instead I ran to bring the news to my father Laban.

Jacob ate with us, of course, and he couldn't take his eyes off me, as I waited on him with a dish of stewed goat's meat. Leah was also in attendance, but he hardly looked at her. Perhaps he noticed her squint, though she wore her veil quite high. I felt uncomfortable: something irregular was going on. In the natural course of things a marriage is arranged as a deal between father and bridegroom, and the older daughter will of course be married before her younger sister. But here was Jacob making it quite obvious that it was me he wanted, not just the family connection. As for myself, I accepted that marriage was inevitable – what else should I do, after all? I couldn't hang about the compound, aging and childless; but I didn't long to be wed, not yet. I was too young. My female bleeding would surely not start for a few years, though Leah bled copiously every month, howling with the pain of her cramps and the frustration of still being single. Our father was keen to get her off his hands and start looking forward to grandsons –and he was already planning how to squeeze the most out of the situation.

I stood by silently, waiting at meals or clearing things away, as little by little Jacob related how, with the help of his mother, our aunt Rivka, he had cheated his brother Esau out of the birthright and their father's blessing. My father realised that he and Jacob were cut from the same block, and he prepared for a battle of wits. The two men eyed each other constantly to seize the advantage. But Jacob had a weak point that Laban didn't hesitate to exploit – he was in love, and needed to gain and keep my father's favour. He agreed to work seven years for Laban in return for my hand in marriage – my entire body, I should rather say, though that's where it stopped. We never talked to each other, except for the merest common formalities, and at the end of those seven years he scarcely knew more about me than he had known at that first meeting by the well. He had spent the time gazing at me lecherously, maybe picturing in his mind what he was not yet permitted to see. But he knew nothing of how I loved to taste the new dates when they were first picked from the tree, or of my abhorrence of mutton fat. When my head throbbed from the hot sun I never felt it was appropriate to tell him, and it never occurred to him to wonder why I was more reticent than usual. Most importantly, I kept to myself my terror of the rites of the wedding night and the bloody horrors of childbirth. Those were not subjects one could ever discuss, not even with one's sister. I pretended to feel as I was supposed to feel, as no doubt many other girls did.

So it's hardly surprising that he suspected nothing when at the end of those seven years my wily father married my sister Leah to him in my place. For days the preparations for a splendid feast were underway, everyone busy with cooking and sewing, but not a word did Laban say to either me or my sister. When I tried to ask him what I should wear for the nuptials he only muttered "Not yet, not now", which I took to mean that he didn't have time to discuss it. Not until the very last minute, when our aunts went to adorn Leah, did I understand.

The next morning I sat quietly by the entrance of the tent in which the marriage had been consummated. My thoughts had been in turmoil all night, trying to get to grips with this new turn in my life story, and I wanted nothing more than to speak to my sister. Jacob was the first to appear. I heard him sigh contentedly and then leap from the side of his bride to go outside and relieve himself. He almost ran into me! For a moment he stared at me in horrified astonishment, and then realization of the trick that had been played on him dawned blood-red. The gods only know why he didn't batter Laban to death that morning; he was certainly strong enough to do so. Maybe the gods prevented it. Who can fathom their wise purposes?

By the way, it was a while before I heard the coarse rumours that I had crouched beneath the marriage bed and murmured amorous words as my sister was deflowered so that the sound of my voice would keep him from suspecting the subterfuge and shaming her[3]. It's the kind of joke which delights camel drivers. Such immodesty would never have occurred to either me or Leah! And surely no new bride would be so brazen as to have indulged in love talk on such an occasion. Anyway,

---

3 *As the midrash on Lamentations asserts.*

how can anyone crouch under a bed? Ridiculous!

After Jacob stormed off to confront his father-in-law I crept into the tent. Leah was sitting up in bed trying not to weep; I glimpsed dried blood on her exposed thighs. "How was it?" I asked timorously. "Not very nice", she said. "But no-one said it would be". That was the last time we ever talked about the intimate act, except later on to wrangle about whose turn it was to be impregnated. Anyway, I didn't have long to wait before I found out for myself. To placate Jacob my father agreed to marry me to him as soon as the celebrations for Leah were over – in return for seven more years of labour, but that's another story.

As soon as Jacob got a taste of copulation he couldn't have enough of it. It certainly suited him to have two wives. Gone was his romantic obsession with me. Banished too was the sentimental dream of a double wedding, Laban's two girls marrying Rivka's twin sons. No, all that mattered now was the breeding of babies, preferably boys. When he had cheated his way into the birthright Jacob had been assured that his father's god would make him into a mighty nation, and he did his utmost to fulfil this prophesy.

Leah outstripped me from the start in the breeding business: in the course of five years she had four thriving sons whilst I was still barren. I was at my wits' end. Leah, with her pack of growing boys, looked down her nose at me. "Why do you even bother going into our husband's tent at night?" she sneered. "He just expends his power for nothing". Even Jacob, who still claimed to love me, taunted me with my inability to conceive, angrily exclaiming that the fault was not in him but in me, and that his god was holding back the fruit of my womb. In my grief and desperation I grasped at a last-ditch resolution. My maid Bilhah had been a wedding gift from my father, so she was my property, and her children would also be mine. Why should I not bring her to Jacob when my turn had come round for nightly intercourse and stand witness as he fertilised her?

Jacob's eyes lit up when he saw the fresh young virgin who would be his bedfellow instead of the second wife whose humiliation was rapidly marring her beauty. And I suspect that his manhood was doubly aroused by my presence as he first deflowered her and then roughly copulated with her again, despite her whimpering. My heart had grown hard with disappointment and humiliation. When Jacob wilted in exhaustion I sharply ordered Bilhah back to the servants'

23

quarters and lay down beside him, embracing him with more affection than I had ever felt before.

The scheme succeeded brilliantly. Nine months later Bilhah gave me Dan, my first son. This was a wonderfully easy way to achieve the honour of motherhood; as soon as it was wise to do so I sent Bilhah to Jacob again, and sure enough, she gave me a second son. After that I desisted: the baggage was growing insolent.

Not content with her own prolific spawning, Leah of course had to imitate me and get more sons via her maid Zilpah, so she had two from her and six from her own body. She was certain that Jacob would abandon me altogether and spend his whole time sniffing round her tent; but then disaster struck: her next pregnancy, the seventh, produced only a girl, Dinah. Leah's winning streak was over. All other things being equal, I don't think she was at all sorry to have a daughter. The household was in noisy turmoil with all those growing boys tearing around shouting, bragging and fighting. I had a constant headache, and started to be very nauseous, especially in the mornings. "If it was anyone else, I'd think you were pregnant", Leah commented sarcastically.

She laughed on the other side of her face when I gave birth to Joseph, my beautiful, clever son, much more beloved to me than the sons I got from Bilhah, much more gracious than any of my sister's crude belligerent boys. He cuddles up to me at night and I stroke his long curly hair, crooning the songs that my nurse Deborah sang me to sleep with, murmuring that he is my little bird, my fragrant unfurling blossom. In the morning he tells me his dreams in his clear confident voice, and together we delve for their hidden meaning. Surely no woman ever loved her child so much. My love is so strong that it's tinged with sickening anxiety. I pray fervently that he'll grow up safe, strong and wise, but oh how I want to keep him as my little boy.

Since escaping from my father, taking the flocks and herds and other property which Jacob insists he worked for, we've travelled from place to place, moving on whenever he receives updated instructions from his God. And now, wonder of wonders, I'm pregnant again. I'd be so pleased to have a settled home, but we're on the road once more. I pleaded with Jacob to wait until I've given birth, but no, his God has to be obeyed. I'm very near my time, and constantly scared of accidents as I sway on the camel's back. To comfort me the midwife says she's sure I'll have another boy, but secretly my lonely heart longs for a daughter.

Stepdaughter

L eah was ten when her mother died. When Laban, the girl's father, noticed that his wife was in a serious decline he married me in the hope of getting male progeny. After that he paid no more attention to his first wife. With the help of our maids, Leah and I nursed her tenderly until the end. Her bodily suffering was acute, and to make it worse her mind was tormented with fear for the welfare of her one surviving child. "Laban doesn't care about her", she wheezed, between wrenching coughs and whimpers of pain. "Please, please, make sure he finds a kind husband for her".

As if I had any influence. Rachel was born soon after Leah's mother died. If she had been a son I might have been able to do something. I had two pregnancies after that, but they resulted only in a miscarriage and a stillbirth. After that I no longer conceived, and Laban stopped visiting me at night or enquiring about me during the day. He put me right out of his mind. Deeply disappointed, he refused to marry again, all his hopes now centring on his sister Rivka's sons, whom he regarded as future sons-in-law: Esau, the elder, as husband for Leah, and Jacob for Rachel.

From the time that her mother became ill Leah wept almost incessantly. She could hardly choke down her meals for crying, and I was afraid that she'd soon go the way of her mother. I did all I could to coax her to eat. "Be well for my sake", I begged her, "and for the baby who'll be here soon". Leah would smile at the thought of having a little brother or sister; she was already very maternal.

Of course, once Rachel was born Leah absolutely doted on her. She held the infant in her arms, rocked her, soothed her when she cried and watched longingly as I bared my swollen breast to feed her. "When I'm married to Esau I'm going to have lots of babies", she said, "And mine will all be sons", she added, half-defiantly. "Then your husband will really love you", I told her, putting my arm round her and squeezing her to me. Poor child, she needed to feel wanted. How blind Laban was, refusing to see his daughters as a blessing.

As Rachel started to toddle, then to walk and then run around the compound, and to babble and then speak, Leah was already glowing with the advent of young womanhood. One day, as her father was walking among the women's tents he stopped, startled. For the first time for years he noticed his eldest daughter, and was stunned by what he saw. That evening he ordered her to wait upon him at supper, and afterwards took her to the chamber where he slept. He kept her there for what seemed a long time, past the time when she ought to have been asleep. Naturally I was extremely concerned. When eventually she ran across the compound and crashed into my tent she was sweating and trembling. "I can't tell you!" she screamed, when I tried to find out what was wrong. "I can't! I can't say it!" But there was no blood on her thighs.

She cried herself to sleep. In the next few days she refused to be comforted and wept intermittently, with snotty, choking sobs. Little Rachel clung to me in uncomprehending distress. Leah's eyes were red and her face puffy with weeping. It's lucky she must always be veiled in the presence of men, I thought. Bit by bit I learnt that her father had stripped her naked, fondled her tender body with his hard herdsman's hands, and made her do things which she could not describe but hid her face in her arms, whimpering, at the memory of.

My mind was made up. As soon as the heat of the day started to wane I took Rachel by the hand and strode out to the pasture, where Laban was talking to his farmhands about the sale of stock. Naturally he took no notice of me, and I was abashed to be a woman alone among rough men, but with a voice only slightly quavering I delivered my message. "Leah is twelve now, maybe thirteen. It's time she had a husband".

Laban turned from the men and the sheep and glared at me, raising his fist. "Mind your own business, woman", he snarled. Seeing I was pregnant, though, he refrained from hitting me, so he couldn't blame himself when his son was born, half-formed and dead, two weeks later.

That was the end of my last pregnancy, and also of Laban's interest in me. I was ill and weak for some time after, and the women of our community brought me food so I could recover my strength, and warm water to wash me. They also brought gossip and news. Esau was married! Without consulting his father, he had taken to wife two Canaanite girls, both daughters of high-ranking men, so he must have grown ambitious to make his own way in the world. To add insult to injury, one of his wives was said to be the daughter of Ishmael, his grandfather's rejected elder son. We heard also that Isaac and Rivka were, naturally, offended and upset by their son's defection. No wonder Laban had reacted so churlishly at the mention of Leah's marriage; for the sake of family peace it was obviously out of the question to seek her union with the man we had always thought her predestined for.

Laban's disappointment was bitter and profound. He had no son, and the son-in-law he had planned for was now denied him. He radiated sullen brutality. Convinced that fate was out to crush him, he took his satisfactions however and wherever he pleased. The women were terrified whenever he approached our tents, especially for their young daughters' sake, hiding them away, and even keeping them from his rapacious grasp by exposing themselves to his lust. Often, however, he was too intoxicated to do much to them except violate their modesty before collapsing into brutish snoring sleep. Leah he regarded as a trophy already won. Despite my constant efforts to protect her he assumed he was entitled to pull aside her garments and paw her whenever he happened to catch sight of her. "Let me give the girl some pleasure", he growled. "She'll be an old maid before any man comes along to marry her". Leah was constantly in tears, her eyes permanently red and watery.

Rachel, though, was her father's pride and joy. She was a lovely, merry little girl, willing and handy at women's work from an early age. She loved to fetch water from the well, and could raise and lower the heavy jug so deftly and balance it on her head so steadily that not a drop was lost. Away she would skip, full of her own cleverness, her eyes shining with delight at being so important and trusted. It was this sparkle of hers, I'm sure, that captured the heart of the stranger.

Well, it turned out that he wasn't a stranger after all but a kinsman. I'm sure you've all heard the story over and over; Jacob was in love, and Laban used his passion as a lever. I have to admit that my husband was smarter than most, and he didn't allow ethical considerations to get in the way of a good bargain. Oh, he could play at being the caring father all right, but he always had his eye on his own advantage. Jacob wanted to be betrothed to Rachel straight away, but Laban demurred. "What's your hurry? She's a child still, nine years old, I think. Wait seven years, get to know the business, and then she'll be ripe and raring to go". And Jacob bought it. He went out into the fields each day, working happily because each day brought the consummation of his love that much closer.

I don't know when the second part of Laban's plan started to blossom in his devious mind. He had given up all thought of Esau coming to claim his destined bride, and with Jacob always around it wasn't prudent for him to go on using Leah in his previous shameful way, except occasionally and surreptitiously. She was becoming a burden. As the seven years drew to a close Leah grew desperate and discontented. She was now at her prime for child-bearing, and she longed to be a mother. Furthermore, it was humiliating to see her younger sister loved and betrothed while she had no prospects at all. But suddenly everything changed, and sometimes a smile was seen to light up her face.

From spurning and scorning his elder daughter when he wasn't fondling her barren breasts, Laban became jovial and kind. He had figured out a neat plan "to please everyone", as he put it when he let me into his schemes – because, of course, as Rachel's mother and the one person Leah trusted I would have an important role to play. So I taught Leah how to sway her body seductively, like her sister, and to imitate the girlish lilt of her sister's voice. I swathed her in the layered wedding robe and veil. When the time came, I gagged Rachel and tied her up in my tent. In one night, whatever love there had been between the sisters came to an abrupt end, as did their trust in me. In obedience to my husband I betrayed my daughter – but what else could I do?

All this happened years ago, and now I'm becoming an old woman shunned by many as sinister and mad. No wonder, no wonder; I can hardly bear my own company. Laban glories in his many grandsons whilst my Rachel remains barren. Estranged from her sister, resented by her husband, terrorised by her rough noisy sons, Leah still weeps, though now she doesn't come to me for comfort. Not long ago, however, she gave birth to a daughter, her little Dinah. Perhaps this innocent child will revive for her the joys of love and intimacy which can only exist between women. This hope sweetens my solitude.

Who Are We?

"What on earth do you mean? I'm Zilpah, you're Bilhah. Who else could we be?"

"Yes, those are our names, always have been, as far as I can recall. But think of those names as words with meanings: Zilpah means 'drooping', and Bilhah means 'faltering, bashful'. Whoever would name their children like that? Come to think of it, who did name us? Our mother, maybe? Do you remember our mother?"

"There were a lot of women, I remember that. You're older than me, maybe you know".

"She was called Hannah".

"That's right, I do remember Hannah. She taught me how to milk the goats and make cheese".

"So you do remember being a child?"

"I remember being little. What's special about being a child, except getting beaten by bigger people?"

"What about our father? Who was he?"

"We didn't really know any men, did we? We saw them sometimes but we never spoke to them".

"Well, that's true enough, but come on, have a little curiosity. Aren't you interested in your origins?"

"Can't say I've ever thought much about it. OK, tell me, who's our father?"

"In the old days, when things were not too hectic, Jacob and I used to have cosy chats. He told me that our mother was married to Ahotay, who had been a captive but was redeemed by Laban – remember him? Laban gave him Hannah for his wife, so Ahotay might be our father. But it's also possible that Laban was himself our father, and that he'd given Hannah to Ahotay so that she'd always be available for him, with a husband who owed him gratitude and would turn a blind eye – men do that kind of thing when they're heads of households".

"How do you know all this?"

"I listen to gossip – not like you, dreaming over the cooking pots. And I put two and two together. It makes sense, doesn't it? Our mother was a concubine, so we were destined to be concubines too."

"And our mistresses are also our sisters in a way? Not in the same way as you're my sister, of course. Well, it's no surprise, now that you come to mention it. I probably always suspected it, somehow. Of course I remember Laban. I wouldn't put anything past him – remember the tricks he played on Jacob? Mind you, Jacob was made of the same stuff as he was. Those men! Always trying to go one better than the other".

"Too true. Do you remember how strange we thought it at that infamous marriage that I, the elder of us two, was given to Rachel, the younger sister, and you to Leah? He must have reckoned that everyone would assume we'd be paired up older with older, younger with younger, so Jacob's suspicions wouldn't be aroused when you, Zilpah, the younger sister, was given to his bride as her maid. Poor Jacob! It just added to his mortification when he realized he'd been fooled".

"He was very angry. I was scared. Leah was unhappy too, but she had the courage to give him what he deserved. He raged at her because of the way she deceived him on their wedding night, answering as Rachel in the dark tent. 'Didn't you answer as Esau when your blind old father called out to give him the blessing?' she snapped. That silenced him. She knew he didn't love her, and he never would. Still, she was lucky that was all she had to worry about".

"You're right, Zilpah. When did we ever imagine that any man would love us? We were content that we had a home."

"Still, Bilhah, I think that in a way Jacob did love us. I know that you were more special to him, because you were Rachel's maid and after she died you were what he had left of her; but he was also fond of me, more than of Leah. He could be himself with us. We were unofficial".

"That's right. He didn't have to worry about favouritism – we weren't likely to be jealous of each other. Rachel and Leah were always on the point of scratching each other's eyes out, poor things. That scheming Laban broke their bond of sisterhood. Why couldn't they have got over it and stayed friends? Remember their squabbles over the mandrake roots, and which of them could have Jacob for the night?[4] They didn't want him for himself, for love, just to satisfy their longing for children, and especially for sons. That was probably Laban's doing too – he could only ever father daughters so I suppose he brought them up to think they had to compensate, give him grandsons. Poor Rachel was desperate when her sister produced one son after another and she was still barren. I remember how annoyed Jacob would get at her continual moaning for children, as if it was his fault. His love for her had sustained him throughout those long hard years toiling for that crook his father-in-law, and he was still driven by it. He only wanted her to love him back, that was all he asked of her, but no, she felt incomplete. Still, it wasn't fair of him to berate her – he had children, but she didn't."

"That's where we came into the picture".

"First me then you. Thanks to me, Rachel got her sons, Dan and Naphtali, two to Leah's four, but then your madam was scared that she'd be left behind and recruited you into the firm. Do you ever feel like a mother? Long for the boys you bore?"

"Me? No – why should I? I was only doing a job. They were never meant to be mine. Leah gave them their names and I never saw them once they were weaned. I wouldn't recognise them now. What about you?"

"My body remembers, sometimes. I recognise an emptiness. She let me keep my daughter, but she's married and gone. Rachel's dead now, and Leah's bitter and strange, since Dinah was raped and her elder sons showed their true colours, shedding all that blood in beastly vengeance."[5]

"So much grief for Jacob. We know about it. Who else could he pour out his heart to? He told us that his mother was ambitious and thwarted. He'd heard that she conceived her twins after years of barrenness, and the pregnancy almost killed her. Then nothing. I can't

---

4 *Genesis 30:15–16*
5 *For the rape of Dinah by Shechem, and the completely disproportionate revenge taken by her brothers Simeon and Levi, see the account in Genesis 34.*

help wondering why. Perhaps her body was damaged by the double birth?"

"Or perhaps her husband couldn't summon up interest in her any more. He was no match for her – Jacob only remembers his father as old and ailing. He lay on his deathbed for countless years – may still be lying there, with Rivka gnashing her teeth in frustration. She was as bad as her brother Laban – and what was the consequence of all her scheming? She lost both her sons, and alienated them from each other. Esau did alright for himself anyway. He was better off without Leah and the rest of this crooked family. What was Isaac's blessing worth, when it came down to it? Jacob was betrayed by Laban, wrangled over by his wives and grieved by his haughty violent sons".

"I feared that he would die of anguish when Joseph was lost, torn by wild beasts they said, but who knows? I wouldn't put anything past those sons of Leah."

"It was heartrending to watch Jacob grow old and hopeless. What joy did it bring him that he had all those sons – your madam's sons? Rachel's sons were the ones he loved, and they brought him terrible anguish. How he suffered, losing Joseph, and losing Rachel when Benjamin was born, having to bury her by the roadside. And as if that wasn't enough, the arrogance and insolence of Reuben, his firstborn, sneaking into my bed at night as I slept, taking me as if his father no longer counted[6]. My own eldest sister's son! The half-brother of the children I bore for his aunt Rachel, ravishing me whilst we were still mourning her! Thank heavens I was too old to conceive; otherwise I would have murdered the babe before it saw the light of day. You know I have ways. The final blow came when he removed Jacob's bed from my tent and set it up in Leah's, perpetuating the old rivalry between the sisters even after Rachel's death."

"If he'd been able to have his own way Jacob would have settled down to a peaceful life with Rachel and been happy, as the old story tells us that Adam and Eve were happy in Eden. He was so much in love with her! Don't you remember how he'd go out into the pasturelands as soon as dawn cast its first shy gleam, singing lustily, with the light of hopeful determination in his eyes? It gave us little girls a glimpse of other possibilities, something to long for. But it was just a story and a dream. For all Jacob's passion, for all his cunning, despite the

---

6 *Genesis 35:22*

birthright and blessing, the course of his days was twisted awry by the machinations of his self-serving father-in-law. He was turned into a breeding stud. His love was corrupted. His spirit was defeated by the life he was forced to live. We know, we've heard his bitter tales."

"He never talks to us now. He's become a stranger, wandering alone for days in search of angels, always hoping for a new divine message that will make sense of it all. Despite all his wives and sons Jacob is sad and solitary. We have each other, but what he craves is a dialogue with God".

"That God of his has broken his heart".

"He's not the man he meant to be. And we've grown old. Look at me and you'll see yourself. Who cares about old women? And who has ever cared about us except when they had a use for us?"

"Are you feeling sorry for yourself?"

"No, we're better off than many. We're fed. We're not beaten"

"So who are we?"

"We're Bilhah and Zilpah. Faltering, bashful and drooping. We watch, we listen, we obey. Sometimes we remember. Sometimes we try to understand. That's all".

"Still, we did give birth to four of Jacob's sons. That shouldn't be forgotten, should it?"

Part Two

In the Time of the Judges

A Mother in Israel: A Literary-Philosophical Interlude

Deborah was a woman who made it in a man's world. Don't ask me how she became Israel's leader, their war chief and dispenser of justice[7]; maybe there were traditions which the writers of the Bible suppressed, to give the impression that women were invariably subordinate and always had been. The information given in the Book of Judges[8] is that Deborah was a prophetess, that she sat beneath a palm tree dispensing edicts, and that she was the wife of Lappidoth. She is addressed as a mother in (or of) Israel; more of this later. Whether this means that she really was a mother is unknown: none of her offspring is mentioned.

She went right to the top, like Margaret Thatcher, who as we know was indeed a mother; a facile comparison, maybe, but there are points of points of similarity between the two ladies. Both, for instance, liked bossing men about, and both were ready to wage war, though I don't recall that Mrs T actually went out on the battlefield as Deborah did.

---

7   *The term Judges, which is the title of the biblical book she appears in, is misleading: a better translation is Chieftains*
8   *Judges 4*

When she ordered Barak to go forth and slaughter Sisera's army he appears to have demurred: "If thou wilt go with me, then I will go: but if thou wilt not go with me, then I will not go." Even though his army was numerically superior to Sisera's he may have doubted their prowess if they weren't supported by Deborah's charisma. She called his bluff – I will surely go with thee, she says, taking care to assure him that the mission would bring him no honour as the Lord, she foresaw, would sell Sisera into a woman's hand. Not only was she a prophet, she had faith in her girl guerrillas.

When Sisera fled from the bloody assault which was wiping out his army he sought shelter at the tent of Jael, wife of Heber the Kenite, who he credulously thought was his ally. Well, Heber may have been on Sisera's side, but Jael was one of Deborah's Amazons. She lulled Sisera into a false sense of security with her ready hospitality, offering him milk and butter when he only asked for a drink of water. Then she murdered him by hammering a tent-pin through his temples whilst he slept. When Barak came in search of Sisera she proudly proclaimed "Come, and I will show thee the man whom thou seekest" – and there lay Sisera, dead, with the pin in his head, a sure indication of Deborah's prophetic powers and of the unfathomable ways of the Lord.

This tale of female leadership and martial victory is strangely at odds with the generally patriarchal ethos of the Hebrew Bible. The Book of Ruth, whose narrative is set in the time of the Judges, shows no sign of women having administrative or military authority; there, as in the Torah, what power women have is dependent on their cleverness in acting within the accepted parameters, in which they held subordinate positions. And the mystery deepens when we read the episode more closely and realise that there are in fact two different versions of the slaying of Sisera, the first the sober prose account which I have already quoted from and the other in the Song of Deborah and Barak[9].

Despite its name, the Song is actually narrated by a rhapsodic 'I' figure who refers to both Deborah and Barak in the third person as he (or she) recounts the triumph of the Israelites over the Canaanite tribes. The language, form and content of the Song indicate that it is very ancient, and scholars believe that the prose narration in Judges 4 was composed centuries later as an expansion and interpretation of the Song. If this is the case, the figures of Deborah and Jael may

---

9 *Judges 5*

derive from a different cultural context, one which preceded or perhaps existed simultaneously with the patriarchal monotheism of most of the Hebrew Bible.

The account narrated in the Song is not identical with the one we read in the prose version preceding it; for instance, Jabin figures in Judges 4 as the king of Canaan but no mention of him is made in the Song, where Sisera is the only significant Canaanite leader. Furthermore, in the Song Jael's assault on Sisera is embellished with poetic devices and is more violent and destructive than in the prose story. Most significantly, the Song makes no mention of Sisera being slain as he lay sleeping; here the implication is that Jael smashed in his head and knocked him to the ground in one-to-one struggle. According to the King James's Version: "and with the hammer she smote Sisera, smote off his head, when she had pierced and stricken through the temples. At her feet he bowed, he fell, he lay down: at her feet he bowed, he fell: where he bowed, there he fell down dead".

The Jewish Publication Society renders the passage thus:

> She struck Sisera, crushed his head,
> Smashed and pierced his temple.
> At her feet he sank, lay outstretched,
> At her feet he sank, lay still;
> Where he sank he lay – destroyed.

Though the two translations don't quite agree on what exactly Jael did to Sisera's head, they both assert that after her assault on him he fell to the ground before her: she didn't dispatch him as he lay helplessly asleep, as in the prose version. Now, killing a man as he slept is the sneaky kind of thing that could be expected of a woman; the prose narrative keeps the detail of the piercing of the temples but tones down Jael's physical prowess. Is this to present her as more conventionally feminine, less of a warrior? The verse of the Song brings to mind celebrations of the prowess of the hero in epic poetry; but the heroes we are familiar with - Hector, Achilles, Beowulf – are all male. Does the Song of Deborah gesture towards a lost age of female martial heroism?

In the prose version, as we have seen, after the slaying of Sisera Barak comes in search of him and is triumphantly shown his mutilated corpse. In the Song, however, in an abrupt change of scene and perspective which suddenly floods the song with pathos and tragic irony, Sisera's mother is shown peering through the window and wondering why her son is so long returning from the battle. Her ladies try to reassure her, suggesting that his army has probably been victorious and the captains are now dividing the spoils, sharing out the damsels and the embroidered cloth. Sisera's mother attempts to believe them; but the reader knows that he will never return. It is in the Song that Deborah is called a mother in Israel, with an implied contrast between the glorious martial mother and the despair of the mother of the slain enemy leader.

Is the plight of Sisera's mother recounted sympathetically or scornfully? We are ill equipped to enter into ancient ways of thinking and feeling, but perhaps one response need not rule out the other? The Song has an emotional complexity which indeed marks it as poetry rather than historical narrative, and it uses familiar poetic techniques. Its language is laconic and sparse, with a figure of speech known as incremental repetition, that is, a detail repeated with slight variation, as in the account of the slaying of Sisera.

These features are also common in ballad poetry, which derives from pre-modern societies; take, for instance, the ballad of Sir Patrick Spens:

> They hadna sail'd a league, a league,
>   A league but barely three,
> When the lift grew dark, and the wind blew loud,
>   And gurly grew the sea. ...
>
> 'Go fetch a web 'o the silken claith,
>   Another o' the twine,
> And wrap them into our ship's side,
>   And let nae the sea come in'
>
> They fetch'd a web o' the silken claith,
>   Another o' the twine,
> And they wrapp'd them round that gude ship's side,
>   But still the sea came in.

As in the Song, the rhythm and the repetition of a few stark works bewitch the reader and create a space for intense though unstated feelings. And with the same repetitiousness, the same laconic irony as the Song, the ballad conjures up a picture of women waiting for their menfolk to return:

> O lang, lang may the ladies sit
>   Wi' their fans into their hand,
> Before they see Sir Patrick Spens
>   Come sailing to the strand!
>
> And lang, lang may the maidens sit
>   Wi' their gowd kames in their hair,
> A-waiting for their ain dear loves!
>   For them they'll see nae mair.

In both the ancient Near-Eastern song and the late-medieval border ballad, form and language give shape and poignancy to bald fact, imagining the pathos of the defeated and the bereaved as well as the triumph of the mighty. Like the ancient epics, whose emotional scope is similarly wide (think of Andromache and Hecuba, for instance), they originated in pre-literate cultures but once written down became available for later interpretation and application. It seems that the Biblical authors worked backwards, constructing a quasi-historical account on the basis of an ancient song from who knows where, editing its details to suit their own purposes and transposing the female heroes Deborah and Jael to a patriarchal context.

But who was Deborah, and how did she come to be named as one of the Judges of Israel? Prophet, warrior and mother, to me she seems a huge archaic figure torn from a setting which can only be imagined, in order to support a narrative of Israel's God-given military might. How can we determine the truth? Stories are protean. In their many shapes, they are the word of the living God.

So, having settled that matter, let's turn to the Book of Ruth.

Gentile or Jew

I am Ruth, the Moabitess. You can read my story, or at least a story whose title is my name, in the Tanach, the Hebrew Bible. The Book of Ruth is short and packed with incident, and its main characters all female, with one exception. It also features a kind of chorus of unnamed women, neighbours and lookers-on, and so many of the verbs are in the feminine form, which is otherwise unusual in the Tanach, for obvious reasons.

I didn't write it, of course, and whoever did had their own agenda.

The account begins with a man, Elimelech, but by the third verse of the first chapter he's already dead. With his wife Naomi and his two sons Mahlon and Chilion, Elimelech left his home in famine-stricken Judah to settle in Moab. They were what has come to be called economic refugees, and the natives of their adopted country might have muttered to themselves that he ought to have stayed at home in Bethlehem and helped make it truly a house of bread[10] again. They would say that he only got what he deserved. But I never knew him. Orpah and I didn't marry his sons until after his death. However, I was soon aware that the family wasn't exactly popular, and there was a distinct tone of *Schadenfreude* in our neighbours' voices when they commiserated with us on the early deaths of our husbands. But that was long ago, and only hearsay or conjecture. There are few factual details in the written account, so what actually happened is irretrievable.

---

10 *'House of bread' is a literal translation of Bethlehem.*

Can you imagine my childhood? Imagination will have to be your mentor, because I can't dredge up much memory of it, or any that I have language to express. And the word 'childhood' is a sham – we were never children in any way you'd understand. Young maidens learnt women's work from their elders simply by sharing in the everyday toil, so we belonged more to the group than to a family. I remember one woman who may have been my mother, but of a father I have no recollection. His name isn't recorded; but that didn't stop the rabbis, who apparently had nothing better to do all day than make up stories, from providing me with a genealogy. They assert that Orpah and I were the daughters of King Eglon of Moab, and thus of royal lineage, which suited them just fine: a humble girl from the detested nation of Moab could hardly be the ancestress to their glorious King David.

But think about it for a moment: how likely is it that the king of a country would marry his daughters to the sons of a foreign widow? No, I'm afraid that the facts were probably more mundane: Naomi wanted wives for her sons to continue the line and give the family legal standing, but she herself lacked a husband to negotiate a good match, whilst we were not quite young and needed to be married off. Is this true? Well, it's as likely as anything. The husbands we got were no great bargains. Their names say it all: Mahlon means sickness and Chilion means consumptive. They were as alike as two peas in a pod; I hardly knew which was mine and which was Orpah's, and it doesn't matter anyway as neither was able to father a child. This fruitless situation continued for ten years, and then they died, within a week of each other.

So there we were, three women working ourselves sore trying to wrest a living from the scrubby piece of land that our dowries had paid for, with no men and no status. We sold our best goats to buy corn, and the ones that remained were too old to yield much milk. It wasn't difficult for Naomi to reach a decision: she would return to Bethlehem in Judah. The famine was long over, and there was some likelihood that she could find a male relative to redeem Elimelech's property for her. We had grown fond of her over the years – after all, she was the one stable point in our lives – and we wanted to go with her, but for days she urged us not to. Go back to your mother's house, she'd say, over and over again. What a laugh! As if we'd be welcome there.

As we turned the cheeses together Orpah and I puzzled over why our mother-in-law was so adamant that we shouldn't follow her to Judah. Could she be ashamed to return with two Moabite daughters-in-law in tow? Our nation wasn't exactly popular with the Jews, for some traditional affront which I bet many of them had forgotten. But there was another thing too. Naomi seemed obsessed with her inability to provide new husbands for us. It is a law among the Jews that if a man dies without offspring his brother must marry his widow to father children in his name; and Naomi had no more sons. This was an enormous grief to her, because naturally she longed for grandchildren. Kind woman that she was, though, she wasn't rejecting us because we hadn't given her any, but hopefully suggesting that we might yet find husbands among our own people and have our own children. "The Lord grant that you may find rest", she prayed, "each of you in the house of her husband".

In the end Orpah gave in. Alone, with just a skinful of water and a bag of coarse bread, she went in search of our kinsfolk. I never saw her again. I hope she reached safety at a settlement where they gave her a home, but it's at least as probable that she was raped and left to die, or raped and taken captive. She was as aware as I was of the dangers awaiting a woman travelling alone, so why didn't she stay with me? Perhaps she could no longer bear Naomi's misery. Or maybe she truly believed that Naomi would be ashamed of her. Come to think of it, how could Naomi turn her out so blithely?

But the story demanded that Orpah leave and I stay. The rabbis, in their profound wisdom and inability to think beyond simple dichotomies, interpreted Orpah's sad departure as exemplifying heartlessness and depravity in contrast to my chaste faithfulness. They asserted that on the night after she left us Orpah lay with a hundred men and one dog, and being a monster she became the mother of four giants, among them Goliath. It would be a lot nearer the truth if they had told such obscene stories about their paragon David.

Now I was alone with Naomi, and my survival instinct told me that staying with her was my one chance for any kind of future. I did care for her, of course – she was the nearest thing I had to a mother – so it wasn't only rhetoric when I made my famous appeal: "Entreat me not to leave thee, and to return from following after thee; for whither thou goest I will go; and where thou lodgest I will lodge; thy people shall be my people, and thy God my God; where thou diest I will die, and there

Gentile or Jew

will I be buried"¹¹. She couldn't hold out against that, and from then on we travelled amicably together, with Naomi apprehensively preparing me for life among the people of Judah.

The homecoming was hard on her. News travels fast, and by mysterious routes: somehow the inhabitants of Bethlehem had heard that she was on her way back, and many of them turned out to jeer at her, the women especially. "Is this Naomi?" they asked gloatingly. The last time they'd seen her she had been leaving them in the lurch, fleeing the famine with her wealthy husband and two growing sons. Now she returned destitute, unaccompanied save for a strange woman. She answered them with a reference to her name, which means 'pleasant': "Call me not Naomi, call me Marah¹²; for the Almighty hath dealt very bitterly with me. I went out full and the Lord hath brought me back home empty"¹³. But as you know, this homecoming turned out to be fortunate for her after all. God helps those who help themselves; and Naomi proved to have quick wits and luck at guessing.

It was the beginning of the barley harvest, and we needed to eat. The Torah, I learnt, enjoins farmers not to reap right to the edges of the field but always to leave some corn for the poor to glean – so a gleaner I became, in the fields of Boaz, an elderly prosperous farmer. It was a joyous time of year and the mood among the young men and maidens working in the fields was festive. But whilst they laughed and flirted I kept myself apart from them, as Naomi instructed me to do. "You have nothing to recommend you but your good name", she said. "Don't give these people cause to think ill of you".

It was good advice. Boaz made enquiries about me, and what he heard must have awakened his sympathy, because he told his young men to be sure to leave plenty of corn in my way and not to harass me. He even came out to talk to me, and said I shouldn't go to glean in any other farmers' fields but to remain on his land, near to his maidens. I was deeply moved: why should he, the great Boaz, take such magnanimous notice of a mere foreigner, a nobody?

Miraculously, Boaz was also a gleaner, in his own way: from what

11 *Ruth 1: 16-17. King James's Version.*
12 *Bitter*
13 *Ruth 1: 20-21. King James's Version.*

45

he had heard of the meagre harvest of my life he came away with a handful of full ripe grains. In the eyes of this old man whose own story was one of loss and sorrow, I was a wondrous example of *chesed*, of loving-kindness and devotion. He told me about his many children, sons and daughters, who had died one by one, and of the recent death of his dear wife. His family had been wrested from him, just as Naomi's had from her, and in me he saw the possibility of comfort. He made sure that I ate with the reapers, and commanded his young men to let me glean among the sheaves, where the best pickings were, and, again, not to molest me.

When Naomi saw how much grain I brought home to her and heard everything that had happened that day, she asked me whose field I had been gleaning in, and then she understood it all – not just the details, but the eerie underlying pattern. This Boaz was a kinsman of Elimelech's, and thus a redeemer for us: it was his right, and indeed his duty, to redeem Elimelech's property, that is, buy it back at the agreed price from the person it had been sold to when Elimelech and his family had left for Moab. The rules for this were laid out in the Torah, Naomi explained to me. She also hoped that he would become our redeemer in another sense, by taking on the obligation to marry me, the childless widow of his kinsman's son, though this was stretching the text of the Law somewhat.

What should be our next move? Naomi sat outside the hovel we shared, staring fixedly at the hard sky. When she spoke, her words shocked me. She told me to bathe, anoint myself with sweet perfumes and dress in my best, and to visit Boaz in secret as he slept on the threshing floor! All my inhibitions rose within me: how could I square this with Naomi's seeming concern for my reputation? But with this ripple in the narrative I felt the waves of fate pushing me on, as a sandstorm will alter the familiar landscape.

That night I crept fearfully to where Boaz lay stretched out on the threshing floor, exhausted with labour, with feasting and wine. Gingerly I crouched down by him and uncovered his feet, as Naomi had instructed. The man started awake. Terror was in his eyes: "Who's there!" he exclaimed; but when he heard my voice he relaxed. Meekly I reminded him of his position towards us of redeemer. Why should he not have taken me by violence then and there? I must have appeared to him like a loose woman, and this in fact was how I felt. But the man was honourable; or perhaps he was simply too old and tired to take advantage of the situation. Who knows? I prefer to believe that he was in fact a true gentleman, a rarity in the Bible. He understood my plight. He said that he was touched that I'd offered myself to him and not to one of the young men. He remarked too that all the men on his holding knew I was a virtuous woman: this I took as a hint of how we should behave towards each other, and it was deeply consoling to me.

The next morning I was up early, meaning to slip away before any of the people could notice me; but the man was awake too. Before departing for his work he told me to hold out my mantle, and he poured six measures of barley into it. I could scarcely stagger home with so much grain.

Naomi's eyes penetrated me as I entered the hovel with my burden. "How are things with you, my daughter?" she asked, with a sharp edge to her voice. I told her everything that had taken place, and something made me add: "He gave me these six measures of barley saying 'Do not go back empty-handed to your mother-in-law, my kinswoman'." For I was coming to realise that this is Naomi's story as much as it's mine.

After that, everything followed as if it had been decreed. Naomi spoke truly when she said, "The man will not rest until he has finished the thing." Boaz knew of a closer kinsman who must first be offered the privilege of being our redeemer, but when this person heard that I was part of the bargain he declined. He wasn't interested in fathering children in the name of a dead man whom he'd never known, and thus impairing his own estate. But Boaz had no children to offend or deprive by making a levirate match[14]. He called all the people together to witness that he had bought that day all that had been Elimelech's and all that had belonged to Chilion and Malchon, and that furthermore, as he put it: "I am acquiring Ruth the Moabite, the wife of Mahlon, as my wife, so that the name of the deceased may not disappear from among his kinsmen"[15]. It was all according to the book. There was no need for him to say that he had any feelings for me.

So there I stood, redeemed. I kept behind him, my eyes modestly turned downwards, my veil covering my face. I played the part as convincingly as I had played the harlot the night before.

---

14 *i.e, marrying the widow of a deceased brother, as explained above.*
15 *Ruth 4: 9-10*

The elders of the community delivered a formal speech inserting me into the line of the foremothers of Israel: "May the Lord make the woman who is coming into your house like Rachel and Leah, who built up the house of Israel. And may your house be like the house of Perez whom Tamar bore to Judah"[16]. I already knew a little about Rachel and Leah; Naomi had told me some of those old tales as we travelled towards Bethlehem. But who was Tamar? Innocently I asked Naomi to tell me that story too, and when she did my eyes were finally opened.

Judah, one of Jacob's sons, had three sons himself, and married off the eldest, Er, to Tamar. Er died, without fathering children, so Tamar passed to the second son, Onan. However, Onan, like our nameless kinsman, refused to father children in his brother's name. When he lay with Tamar he pulled away from her before the act of generation was complete and spilled his seed on the ground. He died too, and as Shelah, the youngest brother, was still a little boy, Judah sent Tamar back to her father's house to live as a widow till Shelah was old enough to marry. But Judah was afraid that Shelah would suffer the same fate as his brothers if he was made to marry Tamar, so he conveniently forgot about her.

Meanwhile, Tamar was getting more and more desperate. With neither husband nor son she was a non-person, and as she was tacitly betrothed to Shelar she couldn't accept any other offers of matrimony. But her wits were sharp. Being a woman, she had only one resource at her command, and she hit upon a way of exploiting that intelligently and even virtuously. She took off her widow's clothing and, hiding her face with a veil, dressed as a cult prostitute and took up her post by the roadside to entice Judah when he came from the sheep-shearing. In his merry mood he lay with her and fathered a son without giving it a thought. Of course the consequences would have been dire for Tamar if she hadn't cleverly turned the tables on him.

The story is easily available[17]: you can read all the ins and outs of it for yourself. For me, the point was that just as Tamar disguised herself as a prostitute in order to regain her status in society, so Naomi got me to do the same. For women like us, degradation and virtue go hand in hand. Furthermore, I also learnt that Perez, the son of Tamar and Judah, was the ancestor of Boaz; and it is prophesied that my son

---

16 *Ruth 4: 11–12*
17 *Genesis 38*

will be the ancestor of the Messiah. Whenever he finally comes, he had better not despise prostitutes.

Boaz didn't live long after the marriage, not long enough to see the son he had begotten. Maybe that doesn't matter, since legally the boy was Mahlon's son, not his. That I can accept. What I find hard to take is that my status as his mother was also erased. As soon as my child was born the women of the neighbourhood took him from me and gave him to my mother-in-law, proclaiming "A son is born to Naomi!" They even gave him a name, Obed. If you read that book which bears my name you might wonder what became of me once my womb had done its job. I disappear from the story, which concludes with a tally of male names, culminating in David.

The rabbis say that I couldn't die until I had witnessed my descendant Solomon, renowned for his wisdom, pronounce on a dispute between two prostitutes who each had a young child. One of the babies had died in the night, and both the women claimed that the surviving infant was hers. You might be familiar with the story. I certainly know how it feels to be a prostitute, and also how it feels to be denied motherhood of my own living child. I am Ruth, Jew and Gentile, wife and whore, mother and barren. I am the outsider who chose exile, the intimate enemy, the exemplary convert who only hoped to survive. If I was able to live long enough to see my great-great-grandson pronouncing judgement on marginalised women, why should I ever die? My spirit still wanders among outcasts, always searching for my dear sister Orpah, mother of monsters as I was the mother of heroes and sages. Why did she have to be sacrificed? For the symmetry of the tale?

Part Three

Across the Fence

Mass for the Virgin

It's sublime music,
Monteverdi's Mass for the Virgin

but has she ever been asked
if that's what she digs?

Maybe the Holy Mother
prefers a tune she can dance to

unwind to, imagine
the girlhood she might have gone on having?

You've seen her
in Fra Angelico's Annunciation,

her neck twisted shyly
awry from the angel –

is it in modesty?
does she feel unworthy?

overwhelmed by the honour?
or by social awkwardness?

she might have preferred to reject
the offer, but was unsure of the etiquette;

and besides, the story
was plotted from eternity.

Poor Mary, a lot depends on you:
the careers of innumerable

nuns, priests, architects,
organ-makers, homilists,

scribes and inquisitors,
crusaders and mystics;

the entire Christian business
of which you'll be the mistress.

She was too inept
too wet behind the ears

to know how to refuse
to stand up for herself

it meant challenging
the entire Establishment.

It was the same at the inn
of course they wouldn't let her in

all dusty from the road
and about to drop her load –

but even Alice, a girl of seven
knew what to retort in a similar situation:

"Nonsense, there's *plenty* of room"!
Was she mesmerised

by Gabriel's androgynous beauty,
comparing him unfavourably

to her elderly betrothed,
and flustered by the pigeon?

I remember the badges:
Don't do it Di!

Common sense couldn't help either lady:
they held no copyright on their virginity.

The pathos of narrative!
The price exacted by stories!

The sheer inhumanity
of sublimity.

Martha's Tale

We were sisters, myself and Mary. I had the reputation of being a real *balabusta*, an excellent housewife who'd be a catch one day for a man who's going places, upwardly mobile, dedicated to his profession; a scribe, a wealthy merchant, a fashionable physician, maybe even a rabbi in an affluent community. Perhaps I sometimes seemed a little too punctilious about my housekeeping standards: I was always dusting, sweeping, polishing, arms up to the elbows in soap-suds when friends called round unexpectedly. My vegetables were always peeled and chopped well before it was time to start cooking, my cakes freshly baked when visitors called. If this zealousness was a fault it was one which most men would overlook, if they even noticed it.

Mary was different. Sprightly as a sprat she was. We both dressed modestly, as Jewish daughters should, but there was usually just a touch of flamboyance about Mary's clothes, some bright trimmings or unusual cut, whilst no-one would give me a second look. They said she was no better than she ought to be, but people will talk, and a lovely, affectionate, open-hearted girl like my sister was the perfect butt of gossip. Mary wasn't in the least domestic. Oh yes, she would do her share if she was reminded, but her eyes just didn't register dirt and dust. If she went to the market by herself, as likely as not she would forget what she'd come out for and return with her basket full of goods that there were plenty of already in the larder. I would scold her, but

I must admit that underlying my exasperation was a smug feeling of superiority.

I mustn't forget to tell you that we were orphans and keeping house for our brother Lazarus. Lazerus, I have to say, was a bit of a stiff. He didn't have his sisters' energy, whether for work, for fun or for the kind of positive contemplation which was Mary's forte, though he was pretty good at mooning about uselessly. I was too tied up in my housekeeping, and Mary in her spirituality, to question whether he was quite well.

Strangely enough, his best friend Josh was a real wonderboy, and Josh kept him going: he had plenty of drive and determination, and enormous faith in himself. Unlike Lazarus, Josh was immensely outgoing. He was in politics, a radical, a spell-binding raconteur and a magical rhetorician, able to mix with people from all social levels. I heard that he had actually risen from artisan stock. His father Joseph was a carpenter; though I've heard that there was some scandal about his birth, and it's true that Joseph had kept well out of Josh's upbringing. Some people said, nastily, that angels were still coming down to earth to visit the daughters of men. In one way this was understandable, because there was something angelic about Josh, charismatic, intuitive. Everyone noticed it: some loved him for it, though others hated him.

This is how our day went. I would spring out of bed at first cock-crow, milk the goat and fetch in the eggs. About an hour later Mary would get up dreamily. She would help to lay the breakfast table, and when everything was ready one of us went to get Lazarus up. Usually he lay there like a stone looking as if only the last trump would wake him, but the way to get him to rouse himself was to say, "Come on now, you don't want to be asleep when Josh comes". Because Josh visited almost every day, and seemed to give our brother a reason to keep on breathing.

Of course we were both in love with Josh. Alright, he made a deep impression wherever he went, and could have had his pick of the girls in our neighbourhood, but Mary and I knew him on a day-to-day basis and continued to dote on him. In our hearts we were sure he was destined for one of us; perhaps for both? We knew all about Rachel and Leah, but we each secretly hoped we were Rachel – I know I did, at least.

Josh didn't discourage our devotion; well, he'd hardly be human if he had. All Jews enjoy good cooking, and all men feel superhuman when they see themselves reflected in adoring female eyes. All the same, the purpose of his visits seemed to be men's talk with his friend, and with the companions who often tagged along with him. To Mary and me he was blandly courteous. Looking back, I know that he didn't display any preference for either of us, though at the time we each hopefully discerned symptoms of love and dwelt on them longingly as we lay in bed after the day's labour.

There was one incident which stood out, one occasion when his guard slipped and he showed his hand, just a glimpse of hidden truth, its meaning unclear. I still sometimes debate with myself the exact significance of what we experienced that day, but I know it was a turning point in the lives of my sister and myself.

He had been roaming around the villages with his followers, talking to people, teaching, making speeches, and converting many to his cause. His route ran through our village, and in he came through our door with a whole troop of dusty, ragged, thirsty, hungry but jubilant peasants hanging on his every word. I immediately did as the Torah commands us, and made arrangements to provide for their needs. I was in fact cumbered with much serving, and all Mary did was plonk herself down on the floor by his feet, her eyes drinking in the movement of his lips. In my irritation I marched over to them and said to Josh: "Don't you care that my sister has left me to serve alone? Tell her to help me". His answer was priceless: "Martha, Martha", he said, "you are careful and troubled about many things: only one thing is needed, and Mary has chosen that good part which shall not be taken away from her".

When he said that my eyes were opened. I knew then for sure that far from loving me, the only feeling he had for me was contempt. He was certainly not refusing to eat and drink what I'd put before him, but he despised me for bothering. And I had no reason to feel jealous of my sister, because it was clear that he didn't love her either. He loved himself, and approved of her sharing his feelings. Mind you, it took a while before it sank in for her. The penny didn't drop until she realised that he was too busy talking excitedly to his male followers to take any notice of her passionate gaze. That night we pushed our beds together and clung to each other, feeling abandoned and vulnerable, whilst our pathetic brother desperately struggled to hold his own in the tavern with Josh and his comrades.

This must have been a Wednesday. We didn't see Josh again that week. He celebrated the Sabbath in the desert with his followers – his disciples, as they called themselves, a rabble of fishermen and labourers for whom his words were gospel. Poor Lazarus could hardly swallow a morsel at our Friday evening family meal. He had no heart for welcoming the Shekinah, the Sabbath bride, for his own bridegroom had deserted him. He too saw how callously his friend had been using us, all of us, Lazarus himself being yet another feather in his cap, the mortally sick man kept from the grave by Josh's divine powers. Though Josh did call a couple of times in the following month it was as if he had removed himself from our sphere. He would talk to us but he no longer listened.

How Lazarus managed to live out that month is a miracle. Four weeks later, on the eve of the Sabbath, he turned his face to the wall and breathed no more. The body was removed from our house and buried immediately, before nightfall, and then Mary and I were left alone to try to eat our Sabbath meal, weeping for our brother and speculating fearfully on our future.

During the weeks that had passed since Joshua had delivered that enlightening thunderbolt I had come to understand many things. I loved cooking and keeping the house beautiful, but I didn't need a man to do it for. Housekeeping was my passion, and if I married it would be as if I was living in adultery. I would be happy to keep house for my sister for the rest of our lives, but I knew she had other ideas. She wanted a man, or men: not necessarily for marriage, since her talents didn't lie that way, but for the sake of the spiritual passion which welled up in her when her body responded to the presence of the other sex – she was addicted to that, and grew miserable and restless if that channel of communication with the Divine had been blocked for too long.

I had heard of a house inhabited by wealthy ladies – widows and heiresses – who gave freely to the needy and were attempting to revive the women's rituals which the priests had mostly succeeded in repressing, and I made up my mind to apply there for domestic work. I had always been a deeply religious person myself, but my religion was of the practical sort, not mystical or esoteric, and that was one reason why Josh's remarks had hurt me so bitterly with their scorn for the essence of my being. With these ladies, I believed, my day-to-day domesticity would be understood as inarticulate worship. I told them my tale, and was overjoyed when they welcomed me into their peaceful community.

The one thing about joining them which made me uneasy was the necessity of parting from Mary. I put off the time of my departure because I couldn't believe that she was capable of looking after herself, either physically or morally, and my fears were justified. As day merged into day she became more ethereal and withdrawn, sitting all night at the doorway staring at the stars, scarcely picking at the good meals which I put in front of her. I told her about my plans and tried to get her to talk about what she intended to do, but I hardly got a word out of her. Then one morning she was gone, without taking so much as an extra pair of sandals or a bottle of water. I ought to have been worried, but somehow I knew that she had taken an inevitable course of action and was as alright as she was ever likely to be. In the evening herdsmen brought news that she had gone into the desert to join a cult, Gnostics who had left the world to search for hidden knowledge. She was the only woman among them, but let's not enquire further.

So my family life had come to an end. I was now free to follow the path I had chosen for myself, so somewhat sombrely I took up my situation in the kitchen of my pious benefactors. I entered their house burdened with a sense of mystery: my life of clear rules and commonplace purposes had disintegrated and a void loomed before me to be filled in the years to come by meaning created laboriously from fragments of ideas and spiritual glimpses as I pursued the domestic routine. My heart yearned towards my sister: our quests may not have been so different after all.

From time to time news of her was brought by tradesmen on their rounds. Ultimately unable to sever herself from that great source of spiritual energy, she had soon moved on to the community of desert desperados which gathered around Josh, fanatics who hailed him as the Messiah. Maybe he believed himself that he was destined to save the world; it's the only explanation I can find for his participation in that crazy suicide mission. My sister was with him at the end, though by his mother's side, not his. I haven't heard anything of her since.

The messianic age hasn't arrived. Terrible passions still create terrible suffering; the natural world retains its harshness. Sometimes rumours reach our peaceful retreat of plagues, massacres, armies which suddenly appear and sack a prosperous city. Some years ago, my household barely survived the annihilation of our harvest by a mighty swarm of locusts: we rationed the stores we had, boiled the bones of our emaciated cattle to make a soup which was thinner every day, even learnt how to eat the locusts themselves. Although we strive to perform his commandments, worshipping, fasting, giving to the poor, helping the sick and bereaved, God seems as distant as ever.

All the same, I have come to believe that messages reach us from the realm of divinity, that each of us encounters angels – messengers – and that we all do angelic service unwittingly. We cannot decipher God's text fully as we are ourselves too much part of it. But I feel sure that Josh was an angel sent to my sister and myself, and to others as well, bringing knowledge transcending his own intentions.

About the Author

For much of her life Marlene R. Edelstein has lived in Copenhagen, teaching English Literature at the university and enjoying the alienated life of a foreigner. She has always written poems – her collection *Believe Everything, Believe Nothing* came out in 2011 – but *Matriarchs* is her first extended foray into prose fiction.

As well as teaching, writing and dreaming, Marlene R. Edelstein loves to give readings from her own work and talks on literary topics. She is fascinated by the Bible as literature.